For Rosa Nella, and may she always
climb the right sort of trees ~ N L

For Hannah ~ S M

Copyright © 2007 by Good Books, Intercourse, PA 17534
International Standard Book Number: 978-1-56148-566-6; 1-56148-566-7

Library of Congress Catalog Card Number: 2006026942

Text copyright © Norbert Landa 2007 • Illustrations copyright © Simon Mendez 2007

Original edition published in English by Little Tiger Press,
an imprint of Magi Publications, London, England, 2007.

Printed in Singapore

Library of Congress Cataloging-in-Publication Data

Landa, Norbert.
Little Bear and the wishing tree / Norbert Landa ; illustrated by Simon Mendez.
p. cm.

Summary: When Bertie Bear gets angry and climbs his favorite tree for a good sulk,
he finds that it magically provides him with everything he needs.
ISBN-13: 978-1-56148-566-6 (hardcover)
[1. Bears--Fiction. 2. Brothers--Fiction. 3. Trees--Fiction.]
I. Mendez, Simon, ill. II. Title.
PZ7.L23165Lt 2007
[E]--dc22
2006026942

Little Bear
and the
Wishing Tree

Norbert Landa

Illustrated by Simon Mendez

Good Books

Intercourse, PA 17534
800/762-7171
www.GoodBooks.com

Bertie and Baby Bear were playing.
Bertie was driving his car and Baby
Bear was chasing him.
  "My turn," said Baby Bear.

"No," said Bertie.

"Why not?" asked Mommy Bear.

"It's mine. And, he'll break it," Bertie shouted.

He ran outside,
slamming the
door behind him.

Bertie peeked through the kitchen window. Mommy and Baby were making pancakes for a snack.

Bertie climbed his
favorite tree and sat
on a leafy branch.
  "I'm going to stay here
all night," he said.

Bertie's tummy rumbled.
He was very hungry! A squirrel
brought him some berries to eat.
But they weren't enough food
for a hungry bear.

Then Bertie spotted the pancake on a branch!
"I didn't know this was a pancake tree," he said.
Bertie ate a stack of pancakes. "Want some?"
he asked the squirrels. "There are plenty."

The sun set and Bertie hugged
his knees.
"You look chilly," a bird said.
He brought Bertie some feathers,
but they weren't enough to cover
a cold bear.

"Thank you," Bertie
said. "But I'm bigger
than you and . . ."

Then Bertie saw a blanket in the tree!
"Wow! This is a pancake-blanket tree!"
He wrapped himself in the blanket.
"If you're cold, I'll share," he called to
the birds.

Bertie loved the moonlight. But when clouds covered the moon, Bertie was a little afraid. Some glow-worms shared their little lamps. But they weren't bright enough for a little bear who was scared of the dark.

Suddenly, light from a lantern dangling nearby lit the tree. "Ooh, this is a pancake-blanket-lantern tree," said Bertie. "Anyone who's scared can join me!"

But the squirrels and birds had
gone to sleep and the glow-worms
had put out their lamps.

Bertie saw the light of the Bear
House. He wanted to tell Mommy
and Baby about his magic tree.

Bertie gathered the remaining
pancakes, the blanket, and the
lantern and clambered down
the tree. Quietly, he opened
the door to his house.

Mommy Bear gave Bertie a big hug. "Look what I brought you from my pancake-blanket-lantern tree," he said.

"What's a pancake-blanket-
  lantern tree?" asked Baby Bear.
Mommy just smiled.
  "I'll show you tomorrow,"
Bertie said, as Mommy tucked
them both into bed.